**To Barbara Martin,
my prayer partner, writing partner,
and friend.**

(You'll read lots of questions in this book, but only one is answered "no." Can you find it?)

I jump out of bed in the morning thinking, "It's going to be a great day, God! I can't wait to go to the zoo."

If I just think it while I'm staring into the mirror brushing my teeth with both eyes wide open . . .

am I praying?

I search for my red T-shirt but can't find it, so I grab my smiley-face T-shirt instead and say, "That's okay, God. It'll still be a great day at the zoo."

If I say it out loud and clear, all alone in my room . . . am I praying?

If I YELL it because I'm so excited I can't say it quietly,

is that still praying?

Mama drops me off at school and drives away with my lunch still on the backseat of her car. I run after the car whimpering, "Dear Jesus, I won't have anything to eat at the zoo. Please make her stop."

But she doesn't.

Am I praying
when I do that?

My lips won't stop quivering.

Todd laughs at me.

On the way to the zoo, I slide across the backseat of the bus and close my eyes. I let the sun warm my face. I just sit there with the bus rocking me while I wait for Jesus to make me feel better. Is that praying?

If I don't really think anything, but just wait for God, is it still prayer?

The teacher loads us onto the zoo train, and I get stuck all alone in the very back seat while the train whips around curves. If I hang on tight and think about God so I won't feel so scared . . .

am I praying?

The train stops, and I can't get out of my seat quickly enough. The other kids crowd off the train and disappear down the path.

I whisper, "Please help me find them, Jesus."

Am I praying when I say that?

BIRD SHOW

And then I say, "Make the teacher miss me and come find me."

That's prayer, isn't it?

Even if she doesn't come?

I walk around pretending to look at the giraffes, and I sing, "Jesus loves me, this I know." If I concentrate on the words about Jesus to make myself believe he won't let anything bad happen to me . . .

is that prayer?

I keep following the path around, looking at the lions and penguins and talking really quietly to God about how much I want to go home.

Isn't that prayer?

Then I see a clock that says
it's almost noon, and I whisper,
"I already knew it was lunchtime
because of my rumbly tummy,
Jesus. Why aren't you helping me?"
Is that prayer, too? Will he get
mad if I say that?

The security guard finds me and asks if I'm lost. I say, "Yes." The whole time he talks to me I'm sort of listening, but in my mind I'm jumping up and down, shouting, "Thank you, Jesus!"

I'm praying when I do that, aren't I?

The lady in the zoo office taps on her microphone, then announces, "If you have lost a little boy in a smiley-face T-shirt, please come get him." I sit on the couch, staring at a poster. I wipe my nose and tell God I don't know why I'm still scared. Is it still praying when I'm too scared to totally trust Jesus?

My mom rushes into the office and twirls me in a big hug, shouting, "Thank you, Lord, for telling me to bring my boy's lunch!" She's talking to God instead of me, and I'm pretty sure that makes it prayer. Then we hop around, laughing and crying together and praising Jesus, because he kept me safe. We're both praying, aren't we?

I bow my head and thank God for peanut butter and jelly before I take a single bite. I know that's praying, because I always pray before I eat.

We find my classmates over by the elephants, and the teacher and the kids run over and say, "Where were you? We were soooo worried. We looked everywhere!" Todd says he's sorry he made fun of me.

I smile and say I forgive him, then close my eyes and thank Jesus for making him nice.

I know I'm praying then because my eyes are shut at the same time I'm talking to God.

Later that night Mama tucks me into bed and pulls the covers up to my chin, but I'm too tired to whisper my prayers. So she prays, "Thank you, God, for keeping Erik safe." I smile with my eyes half closed and agree with her in my thoughts. Even if I drift off to sleep and don't hear the last part of her prayer . . .
I prayed, didn't I?

Did you find the "no" answer?

Every single question about prayer is answered "YES!"
—because there are lots of ways to pray. But when Erik wonders if God
will be mad at him . . . the answer is "No." God never gets mad at us
when we tell him how we feel. He already knows.

For Parents

Read It Together

Reading Erik's story to your child will provide a fun way for him to learn
about prayer. It will teach him how simple prayer is: Any time he speaks
to God in his thoughts or aloud, he is praying. However, remind him that
simply thinking good thoughts about other people is not prayer. God has to
be in the loop. Your child prays by speaking or listening directly to God.

Talking It Over

Tell your child about some of the ways *you* pray.

Ask him to tell you when he prays. Is it at bedtime? Before meals? When
he feels afraid?

Talk about the reasons for prayer: God answers and helps when we call
out to him, and we get to know him better each time we talk to him.

Taking Action

Think of a specific need you and your child both know and care about.
Decide to pray about it together every day until God answers. Make sure it
is something very specific, so your child will be able to see the answer.

Just for Fun

Decorate a shoe box with construction paper or contact paper. Then
whenever you or your child recognize an answer to prayer, write it on a 3x5
index card and drop it into your "Answers to Prayer" box. Once a week, fish
out a card and read God's answer. Then rejoice and praise the Lord together.